"You are troubled, Uncle?" the younger man asked. Tim had grown tall in the years, his illness healed as much by faith and kindness as by medicine, and although he missed being carried on his father's shoulder, his own benevolence towards children had brought him a new joy, since Tim, of all of us, understood that to share kindness with those in pain is a gift beyond words.

Scrooge turned his head and gazed into the young man's eyes. "Yes," he said.

Also by Torger Vedeler

An Easter Carol

Being a Sequel to Charles
Dickens' "A Christmas Carol"

Torger Vedeler

Altakkme Books

AN EASTER CAROL

First Edition, 2024

Copyright © 2024 by Torger Vedeler

Cover by Getcovers

ISBN: 978-1-936783-17-5 (Paperback)

ISBN: 978-1-936783-18-2 (E-Book)

Altakkme Books

altakkme@gmail.com

I have attempted, as best I can, to use English rather than American spelling for this story, in an effort to remain true to Charles Dickens' original style.

For Ed and Steve

Contents

Chapter One

Christmas

W ell, Scrooge was alive, to be sure. You must have no doubt about that, dear reader, none at all, if the tale that follows here is to have any meaning whatsoever. Scrooge was as alive as a healthy, beating heart, alive as a breath leaving its vapours on a cold winter day, as alive as the man or woman who greets you with good cheer in passing, and whose greeting you remember as proof that there is life and that it is good.

But which Scrooge was so living, you may ask? Well, for the sake of clarity (and in case there might be any others), it was *that* Scrooge, that one you know and are most probably thinking of now. Ebenezer Scrooge was his full name, living and breathing in London, walking and greeting those around him with kindness and goodwill, a man whose smile now was as well-known as his frowns and scowls had been before. This Scrooge was warm, both within and without, his positive disposition being more than mere temperature but in that deeper place that should require no coal, that is fed merely by a cheerful "Hello!", a sincere inquiry into the welfare of another. For to understand this tale that follows, you must also know for certain that Scrooge was a better man in all ways than he had once been, that his warmth now had once been the bitterest cold, his harshness of character now redeemed. For the tale that comes before this one, and one you should certainly seek out with interest, tells us how in a single night the Spirits lifted the darkness of greed and selfishness from Scrooge's soul, and that they had shown him that all men should be held together through bonds of compassion. Better than his word, you see, our Scrooge did all this in charity, and infinitely more, becoming to Tiny Tim like a second father, one who the boy and then young man lovingly called *Uncle,* and Scrooge was also a friend and patron to many more. As good a friend Scrooge was, you see, and as good a neighbour, as any could recall, and to those who laughed at him and made note of the occasional silliness of his new demeanor, well, rather than take offense our Scrooge instead joined in their laughter, knowing that such good humour, directed inward, is as smooth a balm for pain or hardship as there can ever be.

Now, there is a second thing that we must note, and this was the sign. For over the warehouse door it still read *Scrooge and Marley,* as it had for longer than anyone could really remember. In the old days it had likely been indifference that prevented Scrooge from painting out his former partner's name, for remember that in the first seven years after Marley's death Scrooge had been happy to answer to either his own name or Marley's, not caring about the confusion that this might cause. Because of course just as Scrooge was very much alive in those previous days (if cold), Marley was very much dead. Dead as a door-nail, to repeat the popular phrase. Dead and buried.

But now? Some people did still wonder, even after Scrooge's redemption all those Christmases before, why he retained the name of old Marley on the warehouse, the name of the man who *was* still remembered as just a man of business, a man who had lived and then died by his accounts and ledgers of profit, and a man bitter and cold and most uncharitable. And why moreso did Scrooge insist, when at last it became necessary to re-paint the sign, that Marley's name be repainted as well, for all to see? For surely Jacob Marley was not a man who most preferred to recall.

Why, you ask? Well, remember who Marley had been, and who Scrooge was now, the undeniable con-trast. For Scrooge was *alive,* as I said, and Marley, as I shall continue to repeat, was very much *dead.* As a door-nail, door-nails being, apparently, particularly dead. Marley was dead and buried in the nearby ceme-tery, interred deep within the cold soil.

But there is more, too, about all this, that none save Scrooge and Tiny Tim ever knew, for although some say that Scrooge had no further intercourse with spirits, this is not wholly true. Yes, the spirits of Christmas Past and Present and Yet to Come did not return to him. But there was still one deed of good that Ebenezer Scrooge had left undone, one thing that now still troubled the old, redeemed miser, and this deed has its own spirit, who we shall meet presently.

For now, however, let us begin at Christmas. The register of Scrooge's office was complete and updated, the doors therein closed and locked, the shutters secure for the holiday, and his home a place of joy this year as it was in every year since his redemption. Here friends gathered to feed those in poverty, to grant a smile to those in tears or with a frown, even to simply hold a hand and thereby show that a sufferer was not alone. For it was Christmas especially that was held to be sacred in this house, kept in the best spirit by Mr. Scrooge himself. See now his nephew and his nephew's wife, come to call.

"Uncle! Merry Christmas!"

"And a Merry Christmas to you, Fred, and to your beloved wife and family! Welcome!"

Fred's wife, who was long past suspicions about Ebenezer, smiled as the old man took her hand and gave it a gentle kiss, as a gentleman should.

"Merry Christmas!" she exclaimed.

Scrooge admitted the two warmly. "And you both know my lead clerk, Bob Cratchit?" he asked.

"Of course. A Merry Christmas to you!" exclaimed the nephew.

"And you!" Bob answered.

Scrooge took their coats and indicated the fire. "And of course, my other nephew, Tim," he said with pride.

Tim, of course, was now a young man, his crutches replaced by a handsome cane, his smile still bright.

"Of course!" Fred exclaimed. "How are you, fellow nephew?"

"Well indeed!" Tim answered, "Fellow nephew Fred!" And all laughed at this old and happy pleasantry, for the two were indeed like brothers.

The good cheer expanded through the room, and all through Scrooge's home. He had hired several more clerks as his business grew, it being profitable to have a reputation for fair dealings and charity. So why, we must ask, did old Scrooge's face sometimes still fall despite all this joy? Why then was there on occasion still a sadness in his eye? Tim saw, even as punch was poured and toasts to the season raised. Tim always saw. And it was his hand, gentle, on old Scrooge's shoulder, there where together they spooned out helpings of soups and meat and porridge to all who came asking, and then later, as together the two sat and stared at the falling snow outside.

"You are troubled, Uncle?" the younger man asked. Tim had grown tall in the years, his illness healed as much by faith and kindness as by medicine, and although he missed being carried on his father's shoulder, his own benevolence towards children had brought him a new joy, since Tim, of all of us, understood that to share kindness with those in pain is itself a gift beyond words.

Scrooge turned his head and gazed into the young man's eyes. "Yes," he said.

Tim nodded. Having seen this before he had his suspicions, though in kindness did not voice them. Instead he followed with a reassurance.

"You are not the man you were, Uncle. You have said so yourself, echoed in this by all of London. The spirit of Christmas redeemed you those years ago, you say, and I both believe this and know it to be true. You came to my aid and granted me a love I cannot ever hope to repay. You, Uncle, have found and you have lived the spirit of Christmas as few before. God has Blessed You, and Each of Us, Every One."

Scrooge smiled but then sighed, this being heavy. A moment passed between the younger man and the older. "Not Every One," Scrooge said softly.

Tim nodded again. As always he perceived what the rest of us do not, and when the reason came he said in a soft voice: "You are thinking of *him,* aren't you?"

"Yes," Scrooge said. "Yes. *Him.*"

Another Christmas Eve, another Christmas Day. Goodwill, joy, and through it all Scrooge smiled and loved, redeemed and forgave, redeemed and forgiven.

Chapter Two

Marley's Grave

N ow, spring soon came to London, early this year, the skies bright (though the air was still thick with the smoke of industry), coats set away in closets, and in the streets people cheerfully welcomed the pleasant hours of longer days. Scrooge could often be seen out walking, greeting his neighbours, shaking their hands.

"A charity, you say?" he asked the two gentlemen.

"Yes, Mr. Scrooge. But you have already given so much...."

"I can give a little more."

A little more always of this liberality, for Scrooge had long before learnt how to live simply, instead being rich in his heart. And then, one day in autumn and out again for his walk, he passed the graveyard. As graveyards should be this was a quiet and solemn place, one where old stones marked lives once lived, the names on them worn but not by all forgotten, and here and there a few flowers might mark a spot, left as memories. Scrooge halted, his hesitation having no real reason, but this being reason enough. He stepped past the gate, his own memories suddenly there, of that funeral so long before that he alone had attended, standing with the men who had dug the grave, and the clergyman who spoke not from familiarity but out of habit and duty, blessing the one lowered with ritual words.

"Jacob Marley was a good man, honest in his commercial dealings...."

Finally a handful of dirt tossed over the casket, turning and walking away, the day and its meaning soon forgotten, for there was business to be done.

Now Scrooge stood, just stood, before the old tombstone.

"I have never thanked you enough, my friend," he said softly. "I have never forgotten how you came to me and warned me of the Three Spirits to follow, and what caused them to come. I think sometimes...."

Here Scrooge's voice slowed, faltering, then to resume.

"I think sometimes of you, you know, and of the heavy chain, the burden you must bear."

So.

It had all begun with a scolding, when Bob Cratchit reminded him of his commitment to giving him Christmas Day free to spend with his family. The words still stung Scrooge's conscience.

"It's not convenient," he had said, "and it's not fair. If I was to stop half-a-crown for it, you'd think yourself ill-used, I'll be bound?"

But a commitment *was* a commitment, even for the old Scrooge, who then that night had gone home alone, as had been his custom. Sitting by himself in the cold, wearing his dressing-gown and slippers, to eat his gruel.

That night.

"Humbug!"

Then the cellar-door, flying open with a booming sound. The face, the very same.

"Who are you?"

"Ask me who I *was.*"

"Who *were* you then?"

Marley. Jacob Marley, in life your old friend and partner. At first, there had been the easy explanations.

"You may be an undigested bit of beef, a blot of mustard, a crumb of cheese, a fragment of an underdone potato."

But none of these were true. The Ghost *was* Marley, and the words to follow had been sincere.

"Speak comfort to me, Jacob!"

"I have none to give. It comes from other regions, Ebenezer Scrooge, and is conveyed by other ministers, to other kinds of men. Nor can I tell you what I would. A very little more is all permitted to me. I cannot rest, I cannot stay, I cannot linger anywhere."

And then, the final thing. Seven years dead. The chain. No relief, forever to suffer.

"But you were always a good man of business, Jacob."

"Business! Mankind was my business." And then, the fateful words: "I am here to-night to warn you, that you have yet a chance and hope of escaping my fate. A chance and hope of my procuring, Ebenezer."

Three spirits. Christmas Past, Christmas Present, and Christmas Yet to Come. And with the final of these, Scrooge remembered the tombstone, his own name etched thereon.

"No, Spirit! Oh no, no!"

The finger still was there. It still pointed.

"Spirit! Hear me! I am not the man I was. I will not be the man I must have been but for this intercourse. Why show me this, if I am past all hope!"

The hand, the first hints of a change to the rigid finger, a small quiver.

"Good Spirit. Your nature intercedes for me, and pities me. Assure me that I yet may change these shadows you have shown me, by an altered life!"

Now Scrooge watched the tombstone before him, reading slowly the name still there: *Jacob Marley.* And old Scrooge reached out, touching this, feeling the letters beneath his finger. Three words followed, the same three words each time, that he uttered upon each visit.

"Thank you, Jacob."

The tombstone remained silent, as tombstones do. And then in time the sun drew low, and Ebenezer Scrooge, the miser redeemed, turned, beginning his long walk home.

Chapter Three

The Spirit

It had been seven years now since the spirits had come to Scrooge, and therefore seven years since he *had* become a changed man, the better man others now saw and greeted. What fewer still remembered was that this meant that fourteen years had passed since Marley's death, since that old miser's demise on Christmas Eve itself. But Scrooge, Marley's sole friend and partner and again, the only one to attend his burial, *did* remember, and so when the holiday came now of seven years since Scrooge's redemption, he was to be found spreading greater Christmas cheer than even in the years previous, serving food to the hungry, bringing more coal to heat those who shivered from the cold, welcoming all. And if any wondered why this was, they chose not to ask, for Scrooge's goodness was now so widely known that even a great fraction more brought no surprise.

Again the snow fell in London, then melted. Again spring. Now, the holiday of spring is two, these being joined by their history: Passover and Easter. Scrooge had learnt to keep them both, greeting the celebrants as he always did, and he had learnt the stories of both, finally listening for the church bells that Sunday and making it a point to have meals prepared for Jew and Gentile alike, making no distinction between their common faith and humanity, their common goodness. For to him they really were one and the same, each meriting his kindness and charity. And so it was on this day of Good Friday that Scrooge returned early to his home and stood before the door. For a reason we do not know he hesitated, staring at the knocker, and for a reason he himself could not discern, he again remembered that Christmas Eve seven years and a little more ago when there had been Marley's face that greeted him.

Scrooge reached forth and touched the cool metal. There was time to remember, but only a little, for on this eve he had an engagement with Tim, and with the family of Bob Cratchit, whose welcome was always warm and that he was loathe to be tardy for. But now, just now, the knocker stared back.

A few words escaped Scrooge's throat, words unheard by any save himself, again oft-repeated and that you have heard already in this account.

"I have not forgotten, Jacob," he whispered. And he turned the latch and pushed, to step inside.

In time, Scrooge had dressed and selected his hat and cane, and he sat by the open door in an old chair, admitting warm air from outside. The knocker stared back and he watched it again. It was not Christmas, so surely there would be nothing supernatural to expect of it now? "I have done all I can, Jacob," he heard himself say once more, an unexpected tear rising even with this repetition. "All I can."

"Have you?" he heard.

It was, Scrooge thought first, merely the wind, only a spring breeze passing through the doorway. But Ebenezer Scrooge was now not so quick to dismiss spirits as he once had been, and so he leaned forward to regard the knocker more closely. "Who is it?" he asked.

A voice answered, familiar.

"I, Uncle. Tim."

Tim, yes. Come to fetch him for dinner. Scrooge rose to his feet. "Nephew," he said, smiling. "Of course."

Tim regarded him. "Are you all right, Uncle?" he asked. "Your face...."

Scrooge's smile broadened, eyes gentle. "An old memory," he answered. "For I am an old man. But this one is not a thing you should see as consequential."

Now Tim, who was too young to have old memories but observant enough to recognise them in others, nodded and laid his hand gently on Scrooge's shoulder. "But one you clearly do," he said. "Do you wish to say why? You know I will listen." And when Scrooge did not answer, Tim added, "Is it that night? That Christmas Eve?"

"That night," Scrooge told him. "But this is a different day, a different holiday." They took the first steps to go.

Still then, only then, Tim hesitated, his fingers gripping more tightly to his uncle's sleeve. Before he could speak Scrooge stopped also, and both the young man and the elder turned and stared once again at the knocker, and then at one another.

For the face thereon *had* changed.

"Step forth," a voice called, that of neither man nor woman nor child, but in its way all three. "Step forth to face me."

And the knocker was a knocker again, even as before them a spirit stood. Scrooge held his cane up. "To whom do you speak?" he asked in a voice softer than he intended.

"To you, Ebenezer Scrooge," answered the spirit. "And to you, Tim Cratchit." The spirit watched them both, and they hesitated.

"You are not one of the spirits I encountered before," Scrooge told it now. "You are not the Ghost of Christmas Past, or Present, or Yet to Come. Them I have not seen since that fateful night."

"Nor shall you, nor do you need to, for *your* redemption is complete," said this new spirit. "And you, Tiny Tim Cratchit, have no need of their guidance."

"So who, then, are you?" asked Scrooge again. "If neither of us has a need for spirits, why do you come here?"

"For another."

"Who is?" asked Scrooge.

"One you know. One you remember. Each of you now, take my hand. I promise your safe passage."

Now, Tim in his goodness saw this, as did Scrooge in his aged wisdom. There would be no harm, but there was perceived a great need. And so each of them reached out and took the spirit's hands, to be led to where they knew not.

Chapter Four

Marley's Love

The boy sat with others, there in rows before a headmaster, each of them learning their letters and their sums. At first neither Scrooge nor Tim recognised the one they had been brought to observe, and so they turned to the Spirit to ask.

"Do you not know this place?" the Ghost answered.

"I fear that we do not," said Scrooge. "It is a school and these are pupils, yes, with a teacher. But beyond that, what is the school? There are many in England, surely, and both Tim and I have attended such. But not this one."

"Look there more closely," directed their guide. "Do you see that boy?"

They did. He was a quiet lad, intent on his books. He had inquisitive eyes, and gave serious attention to his work. The Ghost indicated this, and then Scrooge nodded.

"Wait! He *is* familiar!" the older man exclaimed. "Is that not Jacob Marley, but a boy?"

"It is."

"I never knew him so young! I only met him much later. He seems a bright, industrious lad."

"He is that also, or was," said the Spirit.

The young Marley completed his exercises, and soon both Scrooge and Tim saw him with the other boys, outside in the fresh spring air, where they played. "He is so different from the man I knew," remarked Scrooge. "Here Marley has such joy, and seems to have many friends."

"All true," said the Ghost. "To have friends is a thing that men may enjoy when they are young, but too often lose as they grow older. Women less often lose this treasure, which is to their credit. I recall that you yourself could be a happy child, Scrooge, and that you, Tim, smiled often and cheered for others, even when you were ill. Do you each remember?"

Both replied that they did.

"And so why should Jacob Marley be any different?" asked the Spirit now.

They left that scene and found themselves in another. Now Marley was a young man, and Scrooge recognised him instantly. "His face, though less mature than it was when I had his acquaintance, is clearly his," he said.

"Some parts of youth are never lost," answered the Spirit, "or at least only rarely and through difficulty."

"Where is he now?" asked Tim.

"An apprentice, doing the work of any young man of his station. Do you remember such work yourself, Scrooge?"

"I do. I apprenticed with old Fezziwig, a man of such kindness that I miss him still."

"Never forget the value of a good mentor," said the Ghost. "Never forget the immeasurable wisdom they can provide."

Marley was keeping notes, adding accounts. Others, like him, also toiled thus at desks in the office. But as Scrooge and Tim watched, they noticed that young Marley seemed distracted, glancing up too often. They inquired about this.

"For everything there is a reason," the Spirit answered. "Watch."

Finally the day and its work ended, and Marley, with the others, put his pen aside. At the door to the office, however, he lingered, and a word escaped his lips.

"Anne."

She was, Scrooge and Tim both noted, lovely. Dressed well, with long hair and delicate features. But more than this, she smiled upon seeing the young Marley.

"Jacob," she said.

Scrooge turned to the Spirit. "Who is she?" he asked. "Marley never spoke of her, not in any of the years of our acquaintance."

"You seem surprised," said the Ghost.

"I am. Look at his eyes, the joy in them as he regards her. Does he love her?"

"Yes, as only a young man can love."

"Then why—?"

The Spirit paused, then spoke. "No man knows another completely, Ebenezer Scrooge," it said. "In all there are corners they reveal to no one, sometimes not even to themselves. Surely you have such, and you also, Tim. They are yours, sometimes great joys and sometimes great pains. Watch Marley now, as he takes her hand."

They did. Marley raised the woman's gloved hand to grant it a short and tender kiss. "You are well?" he asked her.

"Well, yes," she answered. "And still better now that I see your face."

"And I, seeing yours."

Scrooge looked down. "I remember such love," he said.

"It cannot be forgotten," the Spirit told them. "This is its nature. And you, young Tim, will know it someday too. Soon, I think, and in a way unexpected. But more I cannot say of that."

"But if Marley was so happy, how did he become...?" Scrooge's voice faded.

"Love is beautiful," the Spirit said. "But it is not easy. As you yourself know, Scrooge, it can also be bitter. It can require hard choices that you later come to regret. Follow me now."

Again they accompanied the Spirit. This time it did not seem far, and they stood together in a well-kept parlour.

"I do not know this place," Scrooge said. Tim was silent.

"It is the home of a Lord," the Ghost explained. "It is most important to our story, so that you may both understand why things were that now are. Marley never mentioned it?"

"Never. I am seeing that there was much of his past that he kept secret."

"Much indeed."

"Why would he do that?" asked Tim.

"Each of us has reasons," the Ghost said. "For you, Scrooge, do you often speak of your many years as a miser?"

"Not often. I am still ashamed of them."

"And you, Tim, do you tell of your old illness, of your need for your crutches?"

"Very rarely," answered the young man.

"Are you ashamed of them?"

"Not ashamed, but the memories can be painful."

The Ghost went silent for a moment, then spoke again. "Look now; Marley appears."

Indeed he did, a young man as before, only now Scrooge and Tim saw that he seemed agitated. Another man walked with him, this one older, well-dressed, his cane tapping at the stones of the walk.

"So, Jacob," this one said. "You have come to me with a question?"

"I have, Sir," answered the young Marley.

"Very well. Ask it, then."

Scrooge and Tim saw Marley stiffen. Was that a flash of fear that crossed his features? Scrooge wondered, for he could not recall ever having seen Marley afraid.

"Sir," the young Marley said, "I wish to ask your permission to court your daughter Anne, for the purpose of marriage."

The older man stopped, regarding the younger. "You are an apprentice to be an accountant," he said. "Is that correct?"

"Yes, Sir."

"So I ask, do you have a title? Has your family an estate?"

Marley reddened. "No, Sir. But my family is not poor, and I have been called diligent by my employer, who you know. I assure you that Anne will lack for nothing I can provide."

"I do not doubt that," said the father. "But what *can* you provide, Jacob Marley? You know I have been called upon for her hand by another suitor, a man with both wealth and title."

Marley's eyes fell. "Yes, Sir—" he began.

"Then you understand that such a match as you propose is quite impossible. You would do well, Master Marley, to remain in your station, and marry one more suitable. You are a fine young man, I do not doubt, but do not hold your gaze too high."

"I didn't know," said Scrooge. "I never knew."

"You suffered heartbreak also, did you not?" asked the Ghost.

Scrooge looked down. "I did. But mine was my own failing, not the act of another. For I left Belle to pursue wealth and fortune, foolishly not seeing these as false idols. Here Marley sought only the hand of one who loved him. It was not his weakness that tore her from him, but her father's demands, the accusation that he was too poor. How cruel a thing is this? And still he never told me. He buried the pain within himself?"

"Yes," said the Spirit. "He did. And do you remember what he told you about the chain you yourself bore?"

"That it was heavier than even his, for I had added to it after his demise."

"Yes. You forged your own chain. In his love for Anne at least Marley cannot be held to harsh account. He loved, but that love was taken from him. Let us look now further, however, for there is a lesson here, Ebenezer Scrooge, one that too many fail to learn: A cruelty done to you by one does not make it right that you be cruel to still another. Marley did not learn this, and so he forged his chain."

"I didn't know," Scrooge said again, now quietly. "I didn't know."

Chapter Five

In Which Scrooge And Tim Admit Their Weakness

F or a time it stayed quiet. Tim watched his uncle, troubled by how Scrooge's gaze remained down, how the older man breathed slowly.

"Uncle?" the younger asked at last.

"I am here, Tim." Scrooge raised his eyes, and repeated once more, "I never knew."

"How could you," Tim replied, "if Marley never spoke of it?"

"But would I have listened, in any event?" Scrooge now watched Tim, not so eager to forgive himself as the younger man was. "In my own foolishness, my own greed, would it have mattered what Marley said to me? Or did he fear that I would have simply seen him as weak?"

"Only he could say, Uncle."

"And he is gone." Scrooge turned to the Spirit. "Is this the reason for your coming?" he asked. "To remind me of what I cannot change?"

"No," said the Ghost. "There is so much more we have yet to do. Come now, both of you."

Again the two took the Spirit's hands, rising. When next they saw, it was later, and Marley sat at a desk, writing figures. "I know that desk," Scrooge said. "It was in our office. He worked there for many hours, often late into the night, as though he wished not to go home. He would allow no one else to sit at it, and even after his death I could not bring myself to do so."

"Does it remain there still?" asked the Spirit.

"It does."

"And what do you place upon it now?"

"I keep fresh flowers there to honour the season, in his memory. I have since that Christmas Eve when he came to me, when he saved me."

"When he warned you of your own chain, yes." The Ghost regarded Scrooge. "Why do you think he did that, Ebenezer Scrooge?" it asked. "Why, in his pain, his eternal suffering, his deserved punishment, do you think Jacob Marley came to you on Christmas Eve?"

"To warn me. That is what he said."

"But to warn you was the result, not the cause. Remember this, Ebenezer Scrooge and Tiny Tim Cratchit: The condemned have no obligation to aid the living. Their suffering is not lessened by so doing, and there is no gain for them by it. Marley could have simply waited for you to join him in damnation, Scrooge, but he did not. Instead he acted to save you."

Scrooge was silent for a moment. "And yet I cannot even thank him," he then said softly. "He suffers forever."

"He does. What he did for you does not undo the deeds of his own wicked life. It does not lighten even one link of his heavy chain. You have become a better man these past seven years, Ebenezer Scrooge. Jacob Marley never could, and he knows this even now."

Scrooge went silent again, unable to look at the form of his old associate, unable to watch as Marley wrote his figures, as he calculated his sums of gold and silver. Tim spoke then.

"He was failed by love, injured by another's cruelty, and so became what he became?" he asked.

"In part," said the Ghost. "Perhaps that pain and disappointment were the beginning. But Tim, you yourself know pain, likely better than most. And like Marley's loss of his love, you understand that the world does not always present fairly. So I ask you now: When faced with your crippled body, when you watched others run and enjoy good health, how did you think of them?"

"I rejoiced that they were happy."

"Did you?" the Spirit asked. "Always? You are known for your generous spirit, Tiny Tim Cratchit. You are beloved and held as an example of strength, charity and goodwill. But answer truthfully now, for in this place lies do not prosper. When you look at those more able and fortunate than yourself, are you not also sometimes envious?"

Tim looked down, and Scrooge saw as suddenly the rush of shame spread across Tiny Tim's face.

"Sometimes," the young man said.

"Yes?" asked the Spirit. "Give your admission. Scrooge and I will not judge."

"Sometimes I was envious. Sometimes I still am. Fate does not seem fair."

"Indeed. As I said, the world is not fair, not always, and some would even say seldom. We all know this. What do you think Marley would say? What did you once say, Scrooge?"

The words came to the old man as though they were yesterday's. "'It's not my business,'" Scrooge said with bitter regret. "'If they would rather die, they had better do it, and decrease the surplus population.'"

"And were these not also the words of Jacob Marley?" the Spirit asked. "Like you, Scrooge, Marley said such things often. And you may have said them too, Tiny Tim, even if none can or wish to hear, even if only in your heart when you suffer the old pains and frustration from your deformity. Does this make each of you evil? Does this add to *your* chains? Do you each deserve damnation?"

Neither the younger nor the older man spoke. Finally the Spirit reached out to each of them. "Let us leave young Marley to his books," it said. "There is more still to see."

Chapter Six

A Friendship

Marley aged, no longer a young man, his back becoming slowly hunched from hours of work at his desk. With Tim and the Ghost Scrooge regarded him. "This is the Marley I knew," he said. "I recognise him more clearly now."

"And that is your desk there, beside his?" asked the Spirit.

"It is."

The door opened and Scrooge saw his unredeemed self enter. Marley did not look up. Scrooge watched himself sit in his old chair. Finally their respective candles grew low.

"Have you eaten?" the younger Scrooge asked.

"I had some porridge," Marley answered.

"My nephew has invited me to his dinner," said the younger Scrooge. "He extends his invitation to you as well."

"Are you going to attend?" asked Marley.

"I don't know. There is still work to do here."

The older Scrooge regarded Marley, watching the man's eyes. His younger self did also.

"Do you remember this?" asked the Spirit to the elder.

"I think so."

"And did you attend the invitation?"

"No."

The Spirit's voice grew gentle. "Tell me, Ebenezer Scrooge," it said. "What do you remember of the accounts and figures from that night?"

Scrooge still watched himself, regarding the way the younger Scrooge focused on his work. Then the elder said slowly, "Nothing."

"Do you remember *any* of the accounts from those nights when you worked so late?"

"Very few."

"What *do* you remember, from those years?"

The old, redeemed Scrooge did not answer quickly, but when he did there was a sadness to his voice.

"I remember one night," he said, "when Marley and I were tired, and we shared a dinner. We talked a little, and laughed once or twice. That recollection is vivid because normally we did not laugh. But then we were away from our desks, from our accounts. We never laughed while working."

"Let us see this happier moment," said the Spirit.

Now the two men sat together, the remains of their meal between them. "Tell me, Scrooge," Marley said, "do you ever think about what we do?"

"What we do?" asked the younger Scrooge.

"The accounts. The records. The sums we lend and collect."

From where they watched, the older Scrooge listened carefully. Somehow his hand had found that of Tim, who gripped him both gently and firmly.

"On occasion," answered the younger Scrooge.

"Of what value is it?" asked Marley. "The world seems to get no better. There are still so many who have so little."

"We lend others what they need to do their business," said the younger Scrooge. "We extend to them the coin which they cannot raise themselves. We rent them spaces in which to work."

"And we profit."

"Yes."

Marley watched Scrooge. "Is it good?" he asked.

The younger Scrooge regarded his associate. "Good?" he responded. "By means of our loans, the clever man may prosper. His work may grow his business, and he may employ others. They in turn spend and can provide for their families. They are paid what they are worth. Isn't that good?"

When Marley didn't answer the older Scrooge did so for him.

"Yes. Very well. But that isn't enough, my old friend. Profit is not the only way to do good. Please, Jacob, tell him—tell me—that you understand."

But Marley stayed silent. In time the two men paid their debt for the meal and departed.

"Why?" demanded Scrooge. "Why do you show me these things, Spirit? Why do you show them to Tim? I ask again: Have you come merely to remind us of our faults? What cruelty!"

"No," said the Ghost. "Scrooge, when my three brothers, the Spirits of Christmas Past, Present, and Yet to Come visited you those years ago, it was to help you turn away from only the greatest of your errors, not to erase them all or to make you perfect. For none have the right to demand perfection from another. Some flaws will remain, always. It is in seeing these and acknowledging them that you can embrace the true spirit of Christmas, and of every day. This is the wisdom found in all honest faiths. It is in this way that all may see that life is a struggle to be better, to be kinder. It is in this way, Tim, that God can Bless Us, Every One. Come now, both of you. Let us see further the fate of Jacob Marley."

Another candle burning low. But not the office now, not the familiar desks. Scrooge hesitated, then started. "I know where we are," he said.

"Do you?" asked the Spirit. "What place is it?"

"This is Marley's home. I inherited it upon his death."

"Yes. But seldom visited before his demise, even by you, his closest associate."

Scrooge regarded the Spirit. "Was I not also his friend?" he asked.

"I cannot answer that. Anyone may use the word, but true friendship is a thing beyond words. Were you?"

Scrooge went silent. He sensed Tim watching.

"Surely, Uncle," the younger man said. "Surely you were. After all those years together, sharing so much?"

"I—"

Marley sat now, alone in his cold home, the flickers of the candle flame playing in shadows across his face. He had eaten, the remains of a simple meal on the plate before him. He looked at his hands, turning them slowly. His lips moved, but no words emerged. Whatever thoughts there were, these were his own, and the Spirit did not give them to either Scrooge or to Tim.

"He looks so alone," Tim said at last.

"He is," answered the Ghost.

"So then where *is* my uncle? Where is his friend? Where is Scrooge?"

The Spirit regarded the older Scrooge. "Where indeed?" it asked. "On these nights, where would you have been, Ebenezer Scrooge?"

A moment, another.

"At my old home," Scrooge said finally. "A small place, cheap. Alone."

"With all your wealth, with all that you and Jacob Marley earned and saved and profited, neither of you could afford even a few hours to visit the home of the other?"

Again the silence first, then the admission.

"No."

"Not even on Christmas Eve, or on Christmas Day?"

"I was not then the man I am now," said Scrooge.

"And neither was he," answered the Ghost.

A quiet scene. Scrooge saw himself from long ago, standing alone. "Where are we?" his elder self asked the Spirit.

"You do not know this place?"

"No."

"I am surprised. You have seen it before."

"Have I? Surely not."

"And you do not recognise those men and women?"

Scrooge watched these, and then, only through the most distant and unwelcome of memories, did the truth emerge.

"These are the ones shown me by the Spirit of Christmas Yet to Come," he said slowly.

"Yes. And in that vision, what did they do?"

Now the memory, painful, frightening and hard, returned fully to Scrooge. "They bargained for my things," he said. "I had died."

Tim only watched, for this vision Scrooge too had never told even to him.

"Yes," said the Spirit. "They are not the best of men and women, and will bear their own chains in time, though not as heavy as yours would have been, or those that Marley now carries. But look at this other scene, Scrooge, for there you are, alive and standing, and though the gravediggers watch with avarice, they do not yet steal, or they have stolen from the house already. So this is not your own death and burial, is it?"

The old memories rose further. "No," Scrooge said.

"Whose, then?"

"Jacob Marley's."

"With only you in attendance. Had he no family? None who cared? None save you to mourn him? There must have been someone, surely."

Scrooge looked down, then at his younger, unre-formed self. "No," he said. "Marley drove all others away. His body was found alone."

"By whom?"

"By me."

The Ghost went silent for a time. Then it spoke softly.

"How could any man be so alone?" it asked. "How could any be so easily forgotten?"

"Jacob Marley was not forgotten!" Scrooge protested. *"I* remembered him. Even at the height of my avarice, I remembered him."

"But as we have seen, not enough to visit him, not even on Christmas Eve or Christmas Day. So I must ask, and I beg an honest answer. How much did you mourn for your friend and associate, Ebenezer Scrooge? When this man, your only friend, if such he could have been called, died, did even you take a day from your work to honour him?"

The younger Scrooge looked at the casket, then at his pocket watch. "Some," his older self said.

"But not much," the Spirit finished softly, "for there was business to be done, accounts to be calculated, debts to be collected."

Scrooge trembled, and a tear escaped his eye, followed by another. Tim reached for his uncle and held him.

"I was a fool," Scrooge said now. "You are right, Spirit. I was a poor friend."

"But a better friend now," the Spirit added. "Do not forget Bob Cratchit. Do not forget your nephew and the many others you now greet with such kindness on the streets of London. Do not forget those who laugh at you with good nature and whose laughter you modestly join. You have not forgotten the lesson of Christmas, Ebenezer Scrooge, not in all these years. Do not forget that your own chain has long since faded away."

Scrooge raised his head, and he looked at the Spirit. "But it is not enough, merely to keep Christmas," he said. "There is something more I need to do."

"And this is?"

"Jacob Marley."

The Spirit regarded Scrooge, and Tim regarded him also. Scrooge himself regarded the younger Scrooge, watching him turn and step away from Marley's casket. And after this younger Scrooge had departed and the gravediggers completed their grim work, the elder Scrooge faced the Spirit.

"Take me to him now," he said.

Chapter Seven

Scrooge, Tim, And The Spirit Converse

For a moment the Ghost hesitated, regarding Scrooge closely. Tim also watched the older man.

"Is this what you truly wish, Ebenezer Scrooge?" the Spirit asked. "You know Marley's fate; you learnt it when he himself came to you on Christmas Eve seven and more years ago. You saw his chain and you heard his moans. The way ahead now is painful, and not without peril, so I make you this offer: I will return you to your life, and Tim also. You will live in the comfort of your redemption, understanding that you are saved."

"I know all this," answered Scrooge. "But I still ask to see Jacob Marley."

"So instead of a comfortable redemption, you would descend into the depths of pain that old Marley feels?"

"I would. Tim need not go, but I must."

Tim looked at Scrooge. "Where you go, I go, Uncle," he said.

Still the Ghost hesitated. "Be careful, Tiny Tim," it said. "This is no light thing. Jacob Marley's punishment is odious indeed. His misdeeds were many, and they were great. Marley never corrected his wrongs. He was greedy and thoughtless, and thus cruel to the least among men. He only learnt the spirit of kindness too late."

"And so he is damned," said Scrooge.

"Yes."

"And you feel no trouble in your heart from this?" Scrooge demanded. "You can listen to his moans and yet have no pity?"

"I am but a spirit," the Ghost said. "I do not have the gift that men have, the blessing and the curse of feeling.

I neither love nor hate, reward nor condemn. I am not the message, but only the bringer thereof."

Scrooge watched the Spirit, his gaze now close as though to read it. "And this message you bring, that your fellow spirits once brought to me, who is its author? Who is it that decides, who chose to save me but condemns Jacob Marley?"

"The one above all others."

"And where is this one? Whence can I petition?"

The Spirit regarded the Man. "This one is within you, Ebenezer Scrooge, and within all of those around you. It needs no intermediary for the honest heart."

"It is even in Jacob Marley?"

"Yes. But Marley does not see it. He cannot. His eyes are closed, as yours were."

"Yet it was Marley who, unsaved, sent the spirits to me. There must be some good in him, or he would have stayed silent."

"True. But consider this, Ebenezer Scrooge: It is always easier to see the chains that bind another instead of the ones that bind yourself, and far easier to release them. To forgive the one who wrongs you is hard, but to forgive yourself harder still. Consider that it took three spirits to save you."

Scrooge looked down, remembering. When he spoke again it was quietly. "So is Marley's chain truly so heavy, or is his weight merely his own realization of his wrongs?"

"Both," said the Spirit.

A moment passed. Tim watched Scrooge, and for the first time his eyes held fear. But he did not falter, standing close to his uncle. The Spirit regarded them both. "I offer you freedom this last time," it said. "Scrooge! What did Jacob Marley say to you? Recite it! I would venture you have thought of these words often, and what they mean."

"'I wear the chain I forged in life,'" Scrooge quoted. "'I made it link by link, and yard by yard; I girded it on of my own free will, and of my own free will I wore it.'" Scrooge nodded. "You are right, Spirit; Those words have never been far from me since his visitation."

"Then you know that there is nothing that Marley can do to escape his bonds. A deed, once done, cannot be undone."

"Yes."

"And you recall that his visage was most frightening?"

"I do."

"But you would both still descend to see him?"

"We would," both the older and the younger man said together.

"Very well," answered the Spirit, and it reached out to take their hands.

Chapter Eight

The Finding Of Jacob Marley

Their descent began in darkness, and both Scrooge and Tim held tightly to the Spirit's hands. Then, around them, there came sounds, moans and a wailing most fearful, echoing to become still louder.

"What is this?" cried Tim. "Surely not all of these can be old Marley!"

"Indeed not!" answered the Ghost. "Did you think that only Jacob Marley was without the spirit of charity, or of kindness? Indeed, there are some whose chains are far heavier than his! Imagine the heartless king of a nation who launches a needless war, or the minister who lies and defrauds his flock while claiming his own faultless virtue! Imagine the ones who, knowing the wrongs of their cruelest thoughts, embark to act upon them nonetheless, turning them into deeds of murder and rape and torture! For them, I wonder if there can be any relief at all from the dark pits they have created for themselves, or from the heavy chains they must eventually bear? A wrong act is a wrong done, and some things cannot be forgiven by even the gentlest soul."

"And so you would judge all by even these harsh standards?" asked Scrooge. "What if their cruelty is itself a response to cruelty done to them or one they love? What if they were merely born with an evil soul, made evil by their creator? Has not that creator some responsibility for his creations and their deeds? Or is God himself merely so cruel, claiming to be above responsibility?"

"Some among my kindred say that God is not," the Spirit answered. "Some say, and this is only a legend whose veracity I cannot attest, that in the end the balance of all deeds will be righted, that the actions of men are but one small part of a much greater whole. But I am only a spirit, and that answer I do not have."

They descended further, the two men clinging still more tightly to the Spirit's hands, until finally it spoke.

"We are here, Ebenezer Scrooge and Tiny Tim Cratchit. Look now upon the one you seek."

Marley. Jacob Marley. Even in this darkest place, Scrooge recognised his old friend and associate. Marley moved across the cold ground, stumbling from time to time and stopping only on occasion, clad in his pigtail, his usual waistcoat, tights and boots; the tassels on the latter bristling like his pigtail, and his coat-skirts, the hair upon his head and even his old spectacles raised to the forehead. His body was wrapped in the heavy chain that Scrooge remembered from his visitation more than seven years prior, this clasped about his middle like a tail, constructed of cash-boxes, keys, padlocks, ledgers, deeds, and heavy purses wrought in steel. Marley moved again, dragging this encumbrance, an occasional moan escaping him. Scrooge released the hand of the Spirit, and he stepped forward. "Jacob?" he asked.

The man drew still, but made no response. Scrooge queried again.

"Jacob?"

Now Marley turned his head a little, and his eyes opened.

"Ebenezer?" he asked. And then his face dropped, a painting of more despair than it had carried even before. "You are here? You did not listen to the Spirits? You did not heed them and embrace the charity of Christmas, did not embrace goodwill towards men and women and children? You are like me, damned?"

"Jacob...." Scrooge said, but now his voice failed. *My friend,* he thought. *My old and dear friend.* Then he found himself beside Marley, and his hand extended to just touch the man's shoulder. Marley drew back.

"No, Ebenezer, please," Marley said. "This is too much. Not you also! Please, not you!"

Scrooge found Marley's shoulder again, caressing gently, yet holding it also. "Jacob," he said, "you *did* save me. I heeded your warning. I embraced the spirit of Christmas and goodwill towards all. I became a changed man."

Marley's eyes opened again, regarding Scrooge, and then they grew wet with tears. "Then why?" he asked.

"Why have you come to this awful place, Ebenezer, if you were redeemed? Why, my old friend?"

"To see you."

A moment, and the two men watched each other. Marley moved a bit, and the chain he wore made a sound, a rattle, weary from how he had dragged it for so long. Scrooge reached out and lifted a link, that his friend might gain a little comfort.

"Something, anyway," Marley said. "You were saved by the spirits. That is something."

Scrooge still held the link, feeling its cold metal. "Something," he said. "But not, I fear, enough."

Tim watched the two men, one who he knew like a second father and the other a stranger. And the Spirit watched Tim, seeing the tears in his eyes, for what the Spirit knew that you and I and even Scrooge may not, is this: Though Marley was a stranger, he was also familiar to Tiny Tim, for they both knew suffering, Marley through his chain and Tim through his crippled leg. Tim watched his uncle seek to comfort the man, knowing that there are some injuries that cannot be wholly healed, that we must simply bear, but that also may teach us compassion. The younger man turned to the Spirit.

"They are friends," he said.

"Yes. Scrooge now has many in the world, but Marley no others."

"I wish—" Tim began.

"What, Tim? Tell me."

"I wish I could be Marley's friend."

The Spirit regarded the young man. "Even knowing that when he was alive, Jacob Marley would have cast you out, that you would have been to him merely part of the 'surplus population'?"

"Even then."

The Spirit heard the truth in Tim's words, and knew their honesty. And it bowed its head to the cripple, humbled before him. "Then you have but one test remaining, Tiny Tim," it said. "But I warn you that the next one will be arduous. For now, however, let us watch these two old friends."

Scrooge sat with Marley for some time, neither man speaking. There was little for Marley to say, for what words are there in damnation, in the endless chains of suffering? And as to Scrooge, it did not feel right to be with his old partner and tell him of the joys of his life now, of the happiness that having the spirit of Christmas brought him, since this was only a reminder of what Marley would forever be denied. And so even the banalities so often exchanged by the living were denied to the two of them.

But they *did* sit together, and from time to time Scrooge would make what effort he could, however small, to make Marley more comfortable. At last the damned man spoke.

"They will not let me see much, the guardians here, except sometimes."

"See?" asked Scrooge.

"The living. I think this is perhaps a mercy, or perhaps another torment. For to see the living, would this bring me joy, or pity, or envy? Maybe all of these."

"I wonder if this is always true, Jacob. The young see their elders, and see the benefits of their experience, while their elders see the young and their vigour."

"Are we meant, then, never to be satisfied?"

Scrooge considered this. "But if we become too easily satisfied, do we then cease to strive?" he asked. He thought of the futility of his old greed, and yet also of a new frustration that sometimes vexed him: No matter how many he fed or clothed or warmed, some always still went hungry and in rags, cold. Now, for the first time since his redemption, Scrooge spoke his doubt.

"I try to do good, Jacob, but I can never do enough. There is always more suffering."

Marley watched Scrooge, and suddenly, despite his pain, his gaze held compassion. "You do not need to finish your good works, Ebenezer," he said, "but neither may you step away from them. That was the chief of my errors, the heaviest link in my chain. When I was young I saw so much suffering that I grew blind to it. I was only one man and thought I could make no difference. So all my life I simply strove for wealth, withholding comfort to those in need, even comfort to myself. To protect myself I denied myself. But of what benefit is that wealth now? Because of my frustration, my life became wasted."

Scrooge watched Marley's face. "Not *all* your life," he answered softly. "Once you sought a pure love, one without conditions."

"Love?" Marley asked. "I loved?"

"Anne," Scrooge told him.

Marley stiffened at the name, this sending a rattle through his chain. "Anne," he said. "It has been so long, like another lifetime, another man. She was so beautiful, Ebenezer. I wonder where life took her? I hope she found happiness. How do you know of her?"

"The Spirit showed me. I'm so sorry for what her father did to you, Jacob. You deserved her love, and she yours. To have that extinguished...."

Suddenly Marley began to weep, with deep, old tears from long before. Scrooge reached out, and despite the chain, he embraced his friend.

"What more of my life has the Spirit shown you?" asked Marley then.

"How you withdrew. How you and I became friends."

"I was a poor friend, Ebenezer."

"Poor? You saved me, did you not? You came to me before it was too late, and you told me of the Spirits of Christmas, and now I understand why. You showed me the most sacred thing, Jacob: Compassion. What greater love is there? But for you...." Scrooge's voice disappeared into the endless gloom. From his damned place Marley managed a weak smile.

"Yes," he said. "I did do that. I wonder why they let me? There is always room here for another doomed soul. And once here, no one ever leaves. Your visit is a comfort, Ebenezer. But it will be, I fear, only a short blink in the painful eternity."

Scrooge said nothing. There were no words, nothing to escape his lips that might bring his old friend relief. And as he watched, he saw Marley's gaze fade, his recognition dim. From behind him he heard the Spirit.

"It is time to go, Ebenezer Scrooge. You have been saved by the Spirits of Christmas, and in the world of the living there are many who daily celebrate your redemption. Here, take my hand."

Scrooge looked and saw the Spirit, and saw Tiny Tim beside it. He turned back and saw Jacob Marley, wrapped in his chain, the one he had forged in life. And then Scrooge spoke, this but a single word.

"No."

Chapter Nine

Scrooge is Damned

"Uncle?" asked Tim.

Scrooge turned from where he stood, his hand moving to rest on Marley's shoulder, a link of the heavy chain beside each finger. The words came then, the thing Marley said to him that fateful night so long ago, the beginning of his redemption.

"'A chance and a hope of my procuring, Ebenezer.'"

I have done this for you, Marley had told him, *even from where I am forever damned. I gain nothing by attempting your salvation, but I do it nonetheless. This* was the truth of Ebenezer Scrooge and Jacob Marley. This, more than any other deed or thing, was what mattered. For somewhere, even in the darkest of places, Jacob Marley had possessed the goodness to try and save his friend.

Scrooge spoke now, voice firming, knowing what he must do. "Go back, Tim," he said. "Your kindness and your compassion are needed in the world of men. Go, and spread the true spirit of Christmas, as you have always done. But my place is here, with Marley, with my friend. For I am his only friend, and without me he is alone."

Tim tried to step forward, held back by the hand of the Spirit upon his shoulder. "But *why*, Uncle?" he cried. "Why remain here, when you can do nothing to help him? Why stay in a futile gesture, when there is so much good you can still do in the world of the living?"

"Because in this place I am needed more," Scrooge said. "I am needed by Marley, because he is damned."

"And cannot be saved!" Tim repeated. "The Spirit said so! Think of those you *can* help! Think of all who still need you!"

Scrooge gave the younger man a gentle smile. "And that is why *you* must return, Tiny Tim," he told him.

"You are the light that can lead others from their darkness. Your love cannot be extinguished. Remember your own words: 'God Bless Us, Every One!'" Scrooge turned to the Spirit. "Tell those who made this place that it is wrong," he said. "Tell those who judge so harshly, as I once did, that it is too easy for any and all of us to do so. I will take on Marley's chain. I will bear the burden for his misdeeds. For I know these, and I learnt their consequences all those years ago from the Spirits of Christmas Past, Present, and Yet to Come."

The Ghost regarded him. "But it is not Christmas now, Ebenezer Scrooge," it said.

"I know."

"Once complete, this choice cannot be unmade. Its echoes will be lasting."

"I know that also. Give me Marley's chain."

"No!" cried Tim. "Please, Uncle! No!"

But now the deed was done, and Scrooge fell, suddenly burdened. Heavy indeed were the weights of Jacob Marley, a lifetime's worth.

Tiny Tim fell to his knees, weeping. "No!" he cried, his word now futile. "This is wrong, Spirit! You know it is wrong! Scrooge redeemed himself for his past! He loved all the world! He cared most of all for the least among us! He is innocent!"

"Yes," said the Spirit. "All true."

"Then I reject you! I reject the spirit of Christmas! It means nothing if it only serves to punish a good man, a blameless man! I will not carry it in my heart! I will not do good! Forge my chain, Spirit! Judge and punish me here if you will! For I judge *you,* all the harsher!"

The Ghost went silent. From where he lay now, Ebenezer Scrooge moaned in his new agony. And then Tiny Tim felt another hand upon his shoulder. He turned and looked, and there saw Jacob Marley.

The man's face was different. There was no pain there, only a deeper sadness as he looked at Tim, until a most gentle expression began to emerge. His words soft, he spoke as he never had before.

"He came here for me," Marley said. "I...."

"You did this!" Tim cried. "But for *your* wrongs, Scrooge would not have needed to sacrifice himself!"

"Yes," said Marley. "He gave himself, completely, for me, because he was... is... my friend." Marley looked at Scrooge pulling on the chain. "And he is and will always be your friend also, Tiny Tim. I see now that this love is unchangeable, no matter what either of us does."

Tim wept, and Marley drew him close. Marley wept also, his tears heavy. And at last both of them felt the hands of the Spirit, hearing its soft voice.

"It is time. We must go."

Chapter Ten

Sunrise

A day passed, this being Saturday, and then came darkness before the next. The Spirit stood silent, and Tiny Tim and Jacob Marley sat together.

"What now?" asked Tim finally.

"You must return to the world of the living," Marley answered. "I must go on to where I know not. For my life is still over, even if I bear no chain. I am certain of only one thing, Tim, though I know not how."

"And what thing is that?"

"Love, Tim. I feel it all around me. It fills me and it becomes me. It is the one eternal thing." Marley extended his hand and rested it on that of Tim. "I know you are afraid, my new friend. You wonder how you can go on. I also know that you are angry, and with good cause. For you have seen a great injustice done here, done to a man who had earned his salvation through both words and deeds. And I can tell that in your dark place you see no hope. But listen! There *is* hope, Tim. There is *always* hope. That is the spirit of Christmas, but it is also the spirit of the day which is about to dawn."

Each of them looked at the Ghost, who still stood silent. Tim blinked. "I see London," he said. "I see the city. And there...."

"Yes?" asked Marley.

"Some women there. They do their morning chores."

"Your home, then. I'm sorry that I cannot follow you, Tim." Marley watched the younger man. "I wish we had more time together. I think that there are many things you could have taught me."

Tim regarded Marley. "Could I?" he asked. "After to-night, I feel that I know nothing. I have nothing to teach. What will I do, without my friend and mentor? How will I face each new day, knowing that he suffers forever?"

Marley had no answer. Then he said, "Tim, I will never be far away from you. Know this. Please know this."

The Spirit spoke finally.

"There," it said. "The dawn breaks. The new day begins. Easter."

Tim and Marley turned, and together they saw the first rays of sunlight.

"Look," said the Spirit.

They did. There, but a short distance off, someone was speaking with the washmaids. He was an older man, dressed in a modest coat and hat, familiar.

"Look," said the Spirit again. And then, in a clearer voice, it added, "Go now, both of you. There is little time before dawn will claim the darkness, and you will see me no more. *Go.*"

The darkness around them faded, and Tim and Marley found themselves standing in the streets they knew. Ahead stood the figure, who watched them both.

"My friends," the figure said. "I am so glad to see you again. Please come to greet me."

This voice they also knew, and together they said the name.

"Scrooge?"

"None other," the man replied.

And so they were running, now suddenly eager, and their eyes clouded with tears. They reached their old friend, and they embraced him. There was no chain.

"How?" managed Tim. "Uncle, how?"

"It is Easter," Scrooge answered.

"But the chain?" Marley asked. "What of the chain? Where is the chain that I forged through my folly?"

Scrooge looked at the Spirit, who had begun to fade beneath the growing light. "Tell them," he said. "Tell my dear friends why, Spirit."

The Spirit smiled. "Scrooge did not know," it said. "He assumed Marley's burdens without condition, without hope for more than an eternity of suffering. He gave the highest measure of friendship, and of love. No chains can stand against this, for it is the answer to the final question. *Love* is the reason, the purpose, and the cause. Greater love has no man than that he lays down his life for his friend. Marley is free at last. Tim is innocent and now wise. And Scrooge? To Scrooge I can only bow down in awe. Embrace now, Ebenezer Scrooge and Jacob Marley. For though you will see each other again, it shall not be until Scrooge has lived out the fullest of his years, and Marley has seen all the joys of heaven. And Tim? Tim will be with his dear friend in life, and forever beyond."

The three stood together as the Spirit faded. Then Tiny Tim smiled in purest joy, feeling the words rise both without reason and with every reason.

"God Bless Us," he exclaimed, "Every One!"